Wildfire

Wildfire

Deb Loughead

orca currents

ORCA BOOK PUBLISHERS

Library and Archives Canada Cataloguing in Publication

Loughead, Deb, 1955–, author
Wildfire / Deb Loughead.
(Orca currents)

Issued in print and electronic formats.
ISBN 978-1-4598-1810-1 (softcover).—ISBN 978-1-4598-1811-8 (PDF).—
ISBN 978-1-4598-1812-5 (EPUB)

I. Title. II. Series: Orca currents
PS8573.O8633W55 2018   jC813'.54   C2017-907688-4
C2017-907689-2

First published in the United States, 2018
Library of Congress Control Number: 2018933735

Summary: In this high-interest novel for middle readers,
Dylan tries to find the source of a series of mysterious fires.
A free teacher guide for this title is available at orcabook.com.

MIX
Paper from
responsible sources
FSC® C016245

*Orca Book Publishers is dedicated to preserving the environment and has
printed this book on Forest Stewardship Council® certified paper.*

Orca Book Publishers gratefully acknowledges the support for its
publishing programs provided by the following agencies: the
Government of Canada through the Canada Book Fund and the
Canada Council for the Arts, and the Province of British Columbia
through the BC Arts Council and the Book Publishing Tax Credit.

Edited by Tanya Trafford
Cover photography by Unsplash.com/Ihor Malytskyi
Author photo by Steve Loughead

ORCA BOOK PUBLISHERS
orcabook.com

Printed and bound in Canada.

21 20 19 18 • 4 3 2 1

For my friends
Cathy and Lawrence Kolyn

Chapter One

"Dylan, I absolutely can*not* believe that we're doing this!" My girlfriend, Monica, was sitting across from me in the rowboat with the widest smile on her face. "I mean, do you know how *long* I've been dreaming about it?"

I tried my best to smile back at her as I fumbled with the oars. We had just set out from the dock in a beat-up rowboat.

Why did Monica's mom have to have a friend who lived in a cottage right on the water? *And* had an old rowboat we could borrow? Why, Fates, *why*? I'd never rowed a boat in my life, which was only one of the many reasons I'd been dreading this stupid floating picnic along the shore of the lake.

Another reason was the bird-watching part. Monica had her bird book on her lap, a pair of binoculars around her neck and an actual bird-call thingy in her hand. Her mind was set on studying ornithology at university in a couple of years. I could barely even pronounce the word, let alone give a crap about watching birds!

Kill me now, I couldn't stop thinking. But I knew it was really mean.

"We're so lucky to be living in a small town like Bridgewood that's surrounded by water and trees and sky," she reminded me way too often. "There's wildlife everywhere! Doesn't it make sense to be able to identify at least some of it? It would make me really happy if you would at least give it a try, Dylan."

So now I was trying, with a fake smile plastered across my face. At least it was a nice day. But it was my day off—this was the last thing I wanted to be doing.

"Look! Cool, it's a catbird," Monica said, pointing at some bushes along the shore. "I've never seen one before. Can you hear the mewing sounds it's making?"

"A bird that sounds like a cat?" I said, straining my eyes as I aimed the lens of the awesome digital camera Monica's folks had let me borrow.

I was saving up for a camera of my own. I was hoping to take Media

Studies at college, if I ever got there, and maybe make movies someday. The way I saw it, at least I could practice my photography on this boring bird hunt. But I was still wishing I could be with some of the guys right now, practicing throwing and batting for the pick-up baseball league we'd formed this summer. Monica had promised she would come to my games if I would bird-watch with her. What a trade-off.

"Pay attention, Dylan," Monica said. "I need you to try to row in a little closer to the shore. But don't clunk the oars too much or you'll scare it away."

"Seriously?" I said. "You realize I can barely steer this thing, right?"

"Try," she said. Somehow I managed to guide the rowboat up to the shoreline where there was a nice flat rock to glide up onto. Perfect landing—except for when the bottom scraped against granite, and the bird fluttered away.

"Darn it! Oh well. Thanks for trying." Monica leaned over and patted my leg. "You're actually not so bad at this." Then she sat back and posed for a photo. I caught her awesome smile as she held up her binoculars and grinned.

"This is a good spot for our picnic anyway," she said. "Maybe if we're really quiet the catbird will come back. Keep your eyes on the bushes."

I wasn't really listening. Again.

"*Picnic*, Dylan," she said, nudging me with her foot. "Let's see what your good old gran packed for us in the basket. Your gran rocks," she added. "Did I mention that?"

"Yeah," I told her. "Way too often. But you don't have to live with her and have her in your face all the time. It's like living with two moms, my life with Mom and Gran. Not as much fun as it sounds." I made a goofy face at Monica, and she laughed.

As promised the picnic basket was stuffed with goodies. Gran's trademark tuna-and-apple sandwiches, chocolate-chunk brownies and a bunch of juicy, sweet cherries.

"It's a wonder she still has time for this," Monica said. "Ever since she hooked up with Buddy—"

"Whoa," I said, cringing. "It's my *grandmother* we're talking about. Can we please not discuss her love life?"

"C'mon," Monica said, "she's a grown-up."

"She acts more like a teenager these days. And it's kinda gross," I said. I took a big bite out of my sandwich.

Monica just smiled and shook her head, then bit into hers. And it was at that exact second that we both sniffed the air and whispered the exact same thing:

"Do you smell smoke?"

Chapter Two

"*Yikes*! I *do*!" cried Monica. "For a second I thought I was imagining it, but for sure someone's smoking. In the woods! In the driest summer in ages. All we need is another Fort Mac."

Monica was echoing everyone else in town, especially my gran. The huge fire in Fort McMurray had destroyed thousands of buildings, and hundreds of townspeople had been left homeless. When it came to natural disasters, we had our own live-in reporter. Gran liked nothing better than to spread the word when something grim—flood, fire, earthquake, tsunami—happened in the world. Monica was one of her biggest fans.

Monica scrambled out of the boat and onto the rock before I could stop her.

"Hang on. It could be anyone in there." I tried to grab hold of her arm but she pulled herself loose.

"Shhh," she said and put a finger to her lips. "Come on, Dylan. Let's find out who this loser is."

When Monica had her mind set on something, there was no stopping her. My only choice was to go along with her.

I didn't want to leave that expensive camera behind in the boat, so I slung it around my neck before following Monica into the woods. We pushed our way through the thick layer of underbrush. Within a few minutes we stumbled on a path through the trees. We both spotted it at the same time. Monica nudged me hard in the ribs.

"Check it out," she said close to my ear.

"I know. I see it," I told her.

I'd seen it before, too, but I didn't bother telling her that. Someone had built a shelter by leaning dried branches on an angle against a thick tree trunk. A perfect hiding place for who knows what. And that was where the smoke was coming from.

"One second," I whispered. The structure was so cool-looking that I wanted to take a few photos.

"Are you kidding me? Some jerk's in there hacking a butt," Monica said. "And you stop for a photo op?"

"You're the one who dragged me out here! So I'm taking advantage of it, okay?"

"Do you know how easily that dork could start a fire? I'm going over to tell them to stop! Right now!"

"Wait," I said and grabbed hold of her hand. "Look, I don't want to scare you, but I know for a fact that sometimes homeless dudes camp out in the woods during the summer. And I *know* they don't like being disturbed."

"Oh please," she replied.

"No, it's true. Cory told me he heard about someone who was riding his bike along this path last week. Some creepy guy chased after him, tried to spit on him and warned him to never come near here again. What if *this* is the guy?"

"Don't be ridiculous. It's probably just some stupid rumor."

I knew it wasn't just some stupid rumor. Because that "someone" on the bike was *me*. I had been riding home from Monica's at dusk. And I hadn't breathed a word to anyone because I didn't want to look bad. That weirdo in the worn clothes and the filthy Blue Jays cap, with breath like roadkill, had scared the crap out of me. So I was not so keen on finding out who was hanging out in that shelter. It might be him.

As usual, Monica ignored my advice.

"*Excuse me*," she said in a voice loud enough to scare away any bird within a mile of us. "We smell cigarette smoke. It's not safe to smoke in the woods right now. You could burn down the whole town, you know."

I realized I was holding my breath. I wanted to say, *Are you nuts, Monica?* But I didn't get a chance. Because now we could hear rustling from behind the screen of branches.

And then a deep voice. "Get your nosy butts out of here."

I hooked my arm through Monica's and started yanking her back toward the boat.

"Dylan, *stop* it!" she said way too loud. I cringed.

I didn't want whoever was back there to know who we were. That would just be asking for trouble. But Monica wriggled out of my grasp and marched toward that stack of sticks. I had my cell phone out by then, ready to call 9-1-1. Monica had reached the shelter and was now peering through the cracks.

"*Mason*? What the heck are you doing here?"

No way. Mason Bates, the best ball player in the whole Muskoka region, was hiding out in the forest, sneaking a butt. I felt pretty dumb for being so scared of Mason the jerk.

Chapter Three

Okay, so I guess Mason wasn't really a jerk. He just always seemed kind of full of himself because he was the town hero. And maybe I was a bit jealous about that, like some of the other guys.

Nobody ever bothered much with Mason Bates because he was never around. Ever since he was a little kid he'd been heavy into baseball. Now he was playing for the Ontario Orioles, a league big enough for the scouts to notice. He was busy most weekends, traveling from one tournament to another.

That's why it had been pretty cool that he'd managed to make the Thursday-evening games for our summer league this year—once in a while, at least. And whenever he showed up word got out, and a lot of his fans showed up too.

Sometimes I wondered if all that attention made him nervous—because if it were me, it sure would. He never knew when scouts might be watching him.

Monica pushed some of the branches aside and peered inside the lean-to.

"Are you nuts, Mason? You have a big baseball career ahead of you and you're smoking? Total loser move!" As usual, Monica didn't hesitate to tell it like it was.

Mason came crawling out, then stood up and brushed off the back of his shorts. He looked almost sheepish. Then he spotted my camera.

"No photos, dude," he warned me, holding up one hand.

"No worries, dude," I told him. But I secretly snapped one anyway when he wasn't looking.

Monica shook her head. "So you're hiding out here *smoking* and you don't want anyone to find out," she said.

"Do you think I'm *proud* of it?" Mason was frowning. I didn't often see him frowning. Most of the time he just seemed to have a half smirk on his face.

"Well, you can't be if you're doing it way out here," I said.

"Well, *duh*, O'Connor," Mason said. "Why do you think I'm hiding? I like smoking, get it? It helps me relax. Some of my teammates like it too. There's just so much stress when you're being scouted." He shook his head. "As soon as I get picked up by a college in the States, I'm out of this hick town. But the pressure is intense." He took a deep breath and let it out slowly. "Sometimes I can't even sleep at night, you know."

"Why don't you talk to your guidance counselor? Maybe she can help you out."

Monica was always so logical. That was one of the other things I really liked about her.

"'Cause I'd feel like a total loser. I'm this big sports hero. I don't want anyone knowing the truth. Nobody—not even Ms. Sinclair."

"Huh, I guess you got a point there," I said. "If I were you I wouldn't tell anyone either. They'd all just start judging you."

"*Exactly*," Mason said and half-smirked. "At least *you* get it, Dylan."

"You guys are idiots," Monica piped up. "Your guidance counselor wouldn't blab it, and at least you could get it off your chest. And maybe even quit freaking smoking!"

"Maybe I don't want to get it off my chest. Or quit. Maybe I just want to keep on doing it. So you have to promise to keep your mouths shut, okay? Because if word gets out, then I'll know who blabbed. And the last thing I need is my coach and parents on my case."

I made a zipper motion across my lips and grinned. Mason the Great had actually confided in me and Monica. She was staring at both of us with poison darts shooting out of her chocolate-brown eyes.

"You really are *idiots*," she told us. "Mason, it's totally dangerous to smoke in the woods. It's tinder-dry. Not to mention the damage you're doing to your *health*."

"Wait right there. Don't move." He slipped into the hideaway and right back out again.

He had something in each hand. Plastic beach toys? "Look. A pail of sand from the beach. And a pail of water. I'm a total Boy Scout. I will definitely not start a fire, okay, Ranger Rick?"

He put them down and brushed his hands together. Now he was actually smiling.

"Hmmm. Well, okay, that's sort of good, I guess." But I knew that frown. Monica wasn't done. "So what about your lungs, huh, Mason? And your so-called career!"

"Geez, I'm not gonna smoke forever," he said. "I can quit any old time."

"Ha! Yeah right! I've heard that line before." Monica shook her head and started walking back toward the rowboat.

"Man, your girlfriend is something else," Mason said. "How can you even handle it?"

"Trust me, she's worth it," I said. "Monica's crazy smart and super cool. Well, catch ya later, Mason."

"On the diamond. Tonight," he replied, giving me a high five before I walked away.

Chapter Four

Just like I predicted, as soon as word got out that Mason was coming to the game that night, half the town showed up too.

It was a perfect July evening. Nice breeze sliding off the lake and not a cloud in the sky. Everyone brought lawn chairs, and coolers loaded with snacks and probably beers too. I was pretty sure there was a law against that, but even my mom's best friend (and my godmother), Officer Nicole Vance, was there with her boyfriend. She didn't seem too concerned. Probably because she had the night off and just couldn't be bothered. Gran and Buddy were there, holding hands. It made me cringe. Mom had to work, so her fiancé was keeping her company at the bar. Ever since Brent had popped the question, I'd never seen my mom happier.

All my closest friends were on our team. Cory, Tanner, Logan and even Eliot Barnes, who was a bit older than us. We called ourselves the Bridgewood Badgers, because badgers are such ferocious animals. We weren't really ferocious, but the name worked. Tonight we were playing the Pinevale Pumas, a team from a nearby town. Some of us called them the Pinevale Pukers, just for a laugh. Especially when we lost.

And compared to Mason Bates, none of us had a drop of talent. But whenever he was playing, we were likely to win.

I knew a few guys from the Pumas. One in particular, Jonas Larson, was an okay dude. I used to take guitar lessons with him back when I was about eight and thought I might be good at it if I practiced enough. Turns out I sucked. He did too. We both quit. Now he worked at Granitewood Lodge like I did. He wasn't front desk like me though. He dealt with outdoor maintenance. He had his driver's license and gave me a lift home now and then in his rusty, gray Accord. That was about all we had in common.

"Oh great," I heard Jonas say to another guy as they were walking toward their bench. "I heard Mason Bates is playing tonight. We don't even stand a chance." He kind of gave me a half wave and just shrugged and laughed.

When Mason showed up everyone started cheering. Good night ahead for the Badgers! No doubt about it. But he'd put the rest of us to shame. No doubt about that either.

"Hey, O'Connor," he said, purposely bumping into me. "What's that skinny loser Eliot Barnes doing on your team anyway? He can't even hit the ball. Heard his dad's a real loser too."

What was *up* with this guy? I'd never talked with him much before today. He'd seemed half decent, but now he was acting like a knob. Hard to believe I'd almost felt sorry for him that morning when he was whining about all the pressure of playing ball. And how he "needed" to smoke.

"Eliot's an okay guy. He's got a job at the Scoop Coupe, which is more than you have, right? And that is not an easy gig. Trust me, I know—way too well. And his dad's not a loser. He's just not around a lot because he works in an oil camp out west. But Eliot can take care of himself. So cut him some slack, okay?" I fist-bumped Eliot as he walked past.

"Yeah, whatever," Mason said. "At least I'll have a frigging career. That dude will probably be scooping ice cream for the rest of his life. Good luck with all that." Then he snickered and walked away.

Wow, Mason really *was* a total jerk! It would be so sweet to bring him down a notch. But how could you ever bring down the town's baseball hero?

We won that night. Ten to one. People cheered. No surprise, Mason got a homer every time. I actually managed to hit the ball a few times. Mostly pop flies. But I got to first base twice and to second once. Unfortunately, Eliot struck out every time, and Mason gave him a hard time about it. I could feel my neck burning, but I kept my mouth shut.

Because I had something on him. And maybe it would come in handy someday.

I slept hard and deep that night. All the rowing and ball playing, I guess. At one point I got up for a drink of water and heard some distant sirens. It wasn't uncommon now that all the cottagers were up here for the summer. The "citiots," as some townspeople called them, often hurt themselves doing dumb things like jumping off boathouses in the dark and partying too hard. Sometimes their bonfires got out of hand, although that probably wasn't it tonight, given the fire ban. Could have been anything. I didn't think much of it as I crawled back into the sack and drifted off again.

Friday my work shift started at ten. So I slept in until nine fifteen, then shuffled down the hallway to the table. All the breakfast fixings were set up on the counter, and Mom and Gran were sitting at the kitchen table, sipping coffees and reading the paper.

"You sure slept," Mom said, grinning at me over her reading glasses. "Do you think ten or eleven hours is enough?"

I just crossed my eyes and poured myself a heaping a bowl of sugary cereal.

Gran frowned. "That's not a very healthy lunch for a working boy," she said. "Let me fry you an egg at least or something, Dylan. Maybe a couple pieces of toast with peanut butter?"

Same lecture every morning.

"I told you already, Gran. I get my lunch at Granitewood for free. And it's an awesome lunch. Usually a huge sandwich and a salad. Trust me, I'll be fine until lunchtime."

"If you say so," Gran said and rubbed the top of my head with her knuckles.

The radio was tuned to the local radio station, The Moose FM. A song had just ended, and now the announcer was speaking. I caught the tail end of what he was saying and my ears perked up.

"...*last night's fire in the forest on the shoreline of Bridgewood...*"

"Turn it up, Gran," I said. She did, and we all listened carefully.

"*The local fire department managed to put out the flames before the whole area was ablaze, so there was damage to less than a quarter acre of woodland. Firefighters are reminding local residents and seasonal vacationers that there is currently a fire ban in the entire Muskoka region and much of Ontario. And to be extra vigilant. Most fires are caused by human error...*"

"See, I told you, didn't I?" Gran said. "I'm always warning you and your friends about—" I put my finger to my lips to shush her. But the radio announcer had moved on to another story. Gran turned the volume down.

"I heard the sirens in the middle of the night," I said, frowning. "I wondered what was happening."

Just then the apartment intercom buzzed, and we all jumped. For some reason the hair stood up on the back of my neck. I got up and pushed the button on the intercom.

"Hi, Dylan. It's Nicole. I need to talk to you."

Yep. Trouble had found me.

Chapter Five

"*What*!" I said, turning back to Mom and Gran. "I had absolutely nothing to do with this one. I just told you I heard the sirens. From my *bed*! Geez, you guys!"

"Okay, relax, Dylan," Mom said. "Of course we believe you. It's just that—"

"Yeah, I know," I said. "But honestly, it's got nothing to do with me, not this time. *Quit* staring at me, will you, Gran?"

Gran shrugged and took a sip of coffee. "We'll see," she said and winked at me.

Officer Nicole knocked and walked in. Mom already had her coffee poured. She sat down at the table with us. She didn't even look at me, thank god.

"Guess you all heard about the fire last night, huh," she said. We all nodded. Nicole stared into her coffee mug. "Yeah, it's a weird one, I have to say. How would a fire start in the woods in the middle of the night? Unless someone was down there doing something stupid. Which is hardly a stretch in this town."

"So is that why the police are involved?" Mom said.

"We got a couple of anonymous 9-1-1 calls. So the police had to show up. Officer Donahue was one of the first on scene. It was just off a dirt road, and there's kind of a wide bike path through there. So luckily it was easy for the fire department to reach. They managed to put the fire out before there was too much damage. There are some cottages near there too. Old Mrs. Winston lives in one, and she's not very mobile. Could have been so much worse."

I gulped. It sounded like exactly the same spot we were at the day before, just up from the shoreline where we pulled our boat onto the rock. But someone else had been there too. Mason.

"Well, that's a good thing then, isn't it?" Gran said, smiling.

She patted my hand like she was sorry for blaming me. But I couldn't even look at her. Because I realized that *now* Nicole was staring straight at me.

Mom and Gran realized it too, and their eyes grew really wide. Gran pulled her hand away from mine as if I'd just scorched her.

"Your name came up, Dylan."

I sighed and squeezed my eyes shut. "And why exactly did my name come up when I was home in bed? *Sleeping*! This I *gotta* hear, Nicole."

"Mason Bates gave us your name after I picked him up this morning. Woke him from a deep sleep. Parents both at work. He's down at the station right now. The anonymous tipper gave us Mason's name. So he's in deep trouble. And he swears you can vouch for him."

I gulped. I pushed away my bowl. I stared at the table, then at Nicole.

"I have to leave for work, or I'll be late," I told her. "Sorry, but I just can't help you right now, Nic. They're counting on me."

"I know that. Which is why I already called your boss and told him you'd be a couple of hours late. He said that was fine. They can cover for you until you arrive. So go brush your teeth and get ready. We can chat in the squad car on the way to the station."

"He's not in trouble or anything, is he?" Mom said in that nervous voice I was getting to know so well.

"Of course not, Steph." Nicole squeezed my mom's hand. "We just need to get a statement from him. It shouldn't take too long. Depends on what else is going on at the station right now. It's summer, and all the nutjobs from the city are doing their thing, so you never know."

Gran just shook her head. "Bet you're wishing you'd eaten a better breakfast now, huh Dylan?" she said.

That cereal sure wasn't sitting very well in my gut.

It wasn't a very long ride, but it was long enough for Nicole to explain a few more things. I'd already broken into a sweat that had to be showing big-time in the armpits of my gray Granitewood Lodge T-shirt, making me look crazy guilty for something I had nothing to do with.

"Mason begged me to ask you or Monica to back him up. Of course I chose you, being that you're my godson and all." Nicole cracked a sideways smile. "And of course you usually know way more about these things than she does."

I gave her a sideways grimace. "Yeah, and it's usually *not* my fault," I reminded her.

"Anyway, here's his story. He told us that you caught him having a butt yesterday. And that Monica gave him a really hard time about it. Man, I love that girl! And that you swore you wouldn't tell anyone about it. Is this all ringing true so far?"

"Yeah."

"He told me you met up with him on his bike, behind a dumpster at a plaza."

"Uh...yeah, sounds about right." I clenched my fidgety hands together tightly in my lap. Was this the right call?

"And he swore he would *never* deliberately start a fire. That he's no pyromaniac. And that he sure wasn't down there in the woods *hacking butts* in the middle of the night. That he never goes out there to just *park his ass in that lame shelter* because there's never *any* time to chill, what with his jam-packed baseball schedule. And that his folks can never find out he smokes, or he's totally screwed."

Oh god, Mason. What a freaking *idiot*! "Well, I can't verify that he *wasn't* out in the woods last night, because

I was home sleeping in my own bed," I muttered, maybe a little too fast.

"Hmm. But why would he even mention being in the woods? I mean, if he never goes out there, how would he know there *was* a shelter? And I can assure you that if there ever *was* one, it's pretty much gone now. Stanley did find evidence of some sort of a stick lean-to near a big tree though."

I tried to swallow. I couldn't. "Who's Stanley?" I said.

"Oh, he's the forensic fire investigator. Figures out the point of origin. If any accelerants were used. That kind of thing. He's seen a lot of bad stuff."

We had just pulled into the station when a little blue hybrid pulled up beside us. "Speak of the devil. That's him there."

A big burly guy with a bald head climbed out of the small car. He peered into my window and grinned.

"Hey there, Nicole," he said with a wave. "And you must be the godson, Dylan. I'm Stanley."

All I could do was nod slowly.

"See you in there," he said, turning to walk into the building.

I glanced over at Nicole. She was grinning at me. "You're going to like Stanley," she said.

I wasn't so sure about that.

Chapter Six

We headed straight for the interrogation room. Through the window I could see Mason flopped over the table with his head buried in his arms. There was a paper cup of coffee beside his elbow. It was still full. When we walked in, he looked up at us, bleary-eyed. Clearly this guy was on no sleep. But was he the one who'd started the blaze? And if so, why didn't he just come clean about it instead of building this web of lies? I needed to find out.

"Good morning, boys. Have a seat, Dylan. I'm Stanley Franklin, by the way. Good to meet you." He shook our hands. I hoped he wouldn't notice how clammy mine was.

"So, Mason, I've already heard your story from Officer Nicole," he said. "Anything else to add? Because a lot of it doesn't add up. For one thing, you look pretty tired this morning. And for another, there's an odor of smoke in this room. Did you realize that, kid? That your clothes smell of smoke? Looks like you slept in them too."

Mason just sat there, blinking slowly. "They do?" he said. "That's weird. Wonder why?"

"Bit of soot on your sneakers too, I see." Stanley was frowning now.

He looked like an angry bulldog. "Care to explain that, Mason?"

I looked under the table at Mason's blackened sneakers. *What. A. Freaking. Idiot.*

Mason's green eyes were huge. Now he was wide awake. "I-I...I swear I don't know. I-I..." Then he put his face in his arms again and started to cry. Mason Bates was *crying*. "Okay! So I was out there last night," he murmured without lifting his head. "And yes, I smoked a couple of butts. But I swear I never started that fire. Dylan saw me down by the lake yesterday. He knows I was being careful. Right, Dylan?"

What a total jerk! He was throwing me under the bus after I'd just lied for him by going along with the dumpster story. To my *godmother*! Who was glaring at me right now.

"Yeah, sorry I lied earlier, Nicole. I guess I was trying to protect this jerk's career or something. It was really stupid of me. But guess what. I *can* vouch for him. And yes, he *was* smoking down there. Monica and I both saw him."

I was so pissed that I wanted to reach out and smack Mason upside the head.

Mason looked up. There was something like relief on his face. Stanley just stared at him.

"Tell them, okay, Dylan?" His eyes were pleading now. "About the two pails. With the water and sand. I take them along in my backpack every time to make sure the butts are out. Boy Scout, remember?"

"There were pails?" Nicole said, looking at me.

"Pails," I said, playing dumb. "I dunno. I'm not sure I remember any pails..."

"Come on," he begged. "Help me out here, O'Connor. Do me a solid!"

I really wanted to torture him a bit longer. But it would be way too lame to let him take the fall for arson.

Suddenly someone was knocking on the door. Mason's dad.

"Don't say another word, Mason!" he yelled through the window. We could see another officer trying to subdue him before he yanked the door open.

"My son has done nothing wrong. He was home last night, all night," he said, grabbing Mason's arm and lifting him from his chair.

"Hold on just a sec," said Stanley slowly.

"And just who might you be?" Mr. Bates asked with a sneer in his voice.

I could see Nicole hiding a smile behind her hand as Stanley stood up to his full height. "*I* might be Stanley Franklin, chief investigator from the Fire Marshall's Office. Why don't you take a seat?"

"Does my son need a lawyer?"

"Just sit down for a few minutes." Stanley paused, then smiled. "Please."

Mr. Bates sank into a chair as if all the air had just leaked out of him.

"So here's the thing," Nicole began in a calm voice. "There have been quite a few grass fires in the area already this summer. We've been lucky that nothing bad came of them. And as the weeks and this dry spell go on, the chances of a massive blaze burning out of control keep rising."

As Nicole spoke, Stanley stared down at his big hands, placed flat on the table. When she finished, he looked up at us with narrowed eyes.

"Someone drops a cigarette butt, a match, whatever, anything could happen. And let's face it. Most folks don't have nearly enough respect for flames. Do you know how many cottagers we've had to warn about bonfires? And frigging townsfolk too. Especially kids with too much time on their hands. I've seen way too many bad outcomes. Way too many 'crispy critters' in my lifetime. That's what we call burned corpses, in case you're wondering, boys."

Mason and I both gulped way too loudly. Mr. Bates looked horrified.

"But last night was no accident. Someone started that fire deliberately. We found evidence of an accelerant. Lighter fluid, we believe. Do you realize how serious a deal this is?"

"Okay, I think you've made your point, Stan," Nicole said.

Mr. Bates's face had gone from red to ashen. "Can I take my son home now?" he said.

"Yes," Nicole told him. "We have no further questions for Mason at this time."

Maybe I didn't want Mason to go to jail. But that didn't mean I wasn't still mad about what he'd got me into.

"Hey, wait a sec," I said as Mason and his dad were leaving the room. They both turned and looked at me. "Maybe your dad can help you out with your problem, Mason. All that sneaking out of the house at night to smoke? It can become a bad habit pretty fast, ya know."

Chapter Seven

"So you just let him go?" I asked when the door closed behind them.

"Yeah," Stanley said. "His story's pretty solid, especially after you confirmed seeing him there the day before. I really just wanted to scare the pants off him. And off you too. But nice job throwing him under the bus at the last minute there, buddy."

"Yeah, well, he totally deserved it. And I hope his parents give him a hard time. He may be a big baseball star, but he can also be a huge jerk. He sure was to Eliot Barnes last night. And a couple of other guys too."

"No kidding," Nicole said. "I saw him giving Eliot a hard time during the game." She missed *nothing* in this town! "I still have a few more questions to ask Mason about what he might have seen in the woods last night," she continued, "but I'll give him a chance to let this all sink in first. He's not going anywhere."

"So is this Eliot character the type to hold a grudge?" Stanley asked. "Do you think he'd try to frame Mason if he knew he was hanging out down there smoking? Set him up to get caught? Because if you saw him, maybe someone else did too. That looks like a pretty well-used bike path. We even found a few ramps and pits that kids must use for off-road bike stunts."

My brain was spinning in every direction. They both noticed.

"What, Dylan?" Nicole said. "Do you maybe know something?"

They were both staring at me. "No, but let me ask around," I said. "Right now, though, I really need a ride to work. I'm late enough as it is."

"Done," Nicole said. "You've been helpful as usual, bud." She squeezed my shoulder.

"Nice meeting you," Stanley said, crushing my hand and giving me a wide smile.

I was a bit distracted at the lodge as I checked people in and answered the phone. I couldn't turn my brain off.

Who was the anonymous tipper who had given Mason's name? Was

Mason lying about starting the fire in the first place? Maybe he'd done it by accident, and it had gotten out of control to the point where his pails of sand and water were no help at all. I'd seen it happen myself once, when we were burning our notebooks at the end of school. A huge blaze flared up and started to lick and singe the tree branches above. Nicole had caught us in the act that time.

Or maybe someone else really was trying to get back at Mason—payback, like Stanley suggested. Someone like Eliot Barnes, who was no rookie at petty crime, might be angry enough to do something nuts like that. Except I knew from experience that Eliot was a really good guy at heart. I highly doubted he was behind this.

My bet was still on Mason, some kind of freak accident that he wasn't owning up to. From what I'd seen, he didn't seem to think things through very well. He just did stuff and then hoped for the best outcome. Figured he'd be able to talk his way out of everything. He'd gotten so cocky that he probably felt unsinkable. As I sat there behind the reservation desk, scribbling a dinner reservation into the book, I had a feeling Mason might just be sunk this time. Because he was probably lying through his teeth.

Then the lobby door opened and in seconds Mason was on the other side of the desk, staring at me. He'd changed his sooty clothes and his hair was still wet from a shower.

I was instantly suspicious.

"You here for dinner?" I said. "Or checking in?"

"Ha-ha. Funny, O'Connor. You really crack me up." He wasn't smiling.

"Got a problem? Because now's not a good time. As you can see, I am working. Shouldn't you be somewhere hitting a ball or smoking a butt?"

"Oh yeah, hilarious. So why did you rat me out to my dad?" Mason looked more miserable than angry, and he couldn't hide it behind his bravado.

Ignoring his question, I asked one of my own. "Did you lie about starting the fire last night or what?" I spoke quietly so none of the other staff would overhear me.

His eyes grew wider. "No, I swear," he hissed. "It wasn't me. I actually *heard* someone rustling around in the bushes before the fire started. And you know what? Someone has been sleeping in there. I could tell by how all the dried weeds were flattened out. I started noticing last week. Maybe *that* was who started the fire. And maybe whoever it was got mad because I was using their shelter. So what if they started the fire to get me in trouble? To get rid of me or scare me away."

"That doesn't make a ton of sense. And what about the soot on your shoes?"

"I don't know! Maybe I stepped in a fire pit or something!"

"Well, why didn't you tell the cops any of this?" I shook my head.

"Because what if whoever did it comes after me, O'Connor? I can't risk it! What if they're some kind of nutbar?"

Just then Mr. Hillier called out from his office. "Dylan, can you come in here for a sec?"

"I ratted you out because you need to quit smoking," I said to Mason as I got up. "And because you made me look like a liar in front of Nicole. *And* because you were being such a jerk to some of the guys at the game last night."

"But I didn't frigging *do* anything," he said in an almost whiny voice.

I turned my back on Mason and headed toward my boss's office. I heard the lobby door close. Now I had a whole bunch of new questions jangling around in my brain.

Chapter Eight

After I ran the errand for Mr. Hillier, I sat back at the registration desk and watched the antique clock. I swear it was moving backward. So who had been sleeping in that shelter? Was it the guy who had spit at me last week? One of those homeless vagrants who often camped out in the woods for the summer? Or some kid who just wanted a sleep-out under the stars? Who the heck *was* it? I needed to know. Because maybe Mason was right. Maybe that person had something to do with starting the fire, whether accidentally or on purpose.

And then there was Eliot Barnes. I had already decided to pop into the Scoop Coupe after work and ask him a few questions. I checked the clock again. Only a couple of minutes had passed since the last time I looked. One more dragging hour to go.

Just before six o'clock Jonas stuck his head in the door and offered me a ride into town. At 6:01 I was in the parking lot standing beside his beater. He showed up a few minutes later and tossed his backpack onto the backseat.

It was a blazing-hot July day, and the car was boiling. Jonas opened all the windows and the sunroof. As soon as we were out of sight of the lodge, he lit up a smoke. Just like he always did.

"So I guess you heard about the fire last night," I said, making conversation.

"Who hasn't? Big news in small towns, right? Wonder who it was."

"No clue," I told him. "But they picked Mason up this morning and questioned him." Drat. I regretted blabbing the second those words were out of my mouth.

Jonas looked over at me with raised eyebrows, then turned his eyes back to the road.

"How did they even get his name?" he asked. He took another deep drag off his cigarette, then offered it to me.

"No thanks, not into it. I don't know how they got his name." At least I withheld that much. What a blabbermouth!

"Crime Stoppers tip maybe?" Jonas said, blowing a stream of smoke out his nostrils. "You know, I've seen Bates hiding down there smoking. When I was on my bike, trying out some of those jumps. Lousy spot, right? What a goofball."

"Yeah, Monica and I saw him down there too. Just yesterday." While we were out bird-watching, I *didn't* add. "It's a mystery, I guess. The cops will figure it out. Hey, a bunch of us have retro game nights every now and then. You know, Monopoly, Clue, card games. Maybe you and your girlfriend want to come and chill with us some time?"

"Huh, maybe," he said. "Sounds like something Poppy would be into. Let me know the next time you're planning one."

We had reached the main part of town by then. I got Jonas to stop at the corner closest to the Scoop Coupe. As I was climbing out, I happened to glance down and noticed his boots. Suddenly my throat felt tight.

"What's up, dude?" Jonas said. "Did you leave something at work?"

I gazed straight into his eyes. "Nah, I just thought of something I forgot to do. Oh well."

I slammed the door and knocked on the side of his car as he drove away.

Why was there soot on his boots? Just like on Mason's this morning. True, Jonas worked outdoors at the lodge. Maybe he was working around the fire pits or something. I'd check that out tomorrow. But something else had struck me. Jonas had said, *Wonder who it was.* Not *Wonder how it started?* That seemed odd to me, big-time.

The bell tinkled above the door when I walked into the Scoop Coupe. That had driven me crazy when I worked there. Every tinkle meant more customers. Sometimes I had hardly had a chance to look up from the ice-cream cabinet.

Robbie was behind the counter. The place was always quiet during the dinner hour. It usually picked up again around seven. I frowned. Robbie never scooped. She was usually in the back or else out front, chatting with the customers. Her eyes widened when she spotted me.

"Where's Eliot?" I said. "Didn't he show up for work today?"

The hair prickled on the back of my neck. I'd given him this job, my springtime job, so he'd have more responsibility. *And* to help him get his act together. It wasn't common knowledge that he lived by himself in a rundown little house. And that his dad sent him rent and food money every month from out in Alberta where he was working. But word was getting around. And townspeople judged him because of his background and circumstances.

"Yeah, he was here," Robbie said. "He was supposed to work two to ten. But he had to leave around three."

"Why did he have to leave?" I walked slowly toward the counter. "What happened?"

"Well, Nicole came in with a big fellow named Stanley. They took Eliot aside for a few seconds, and then they told me he had to go with them. For questioning or something. I don't know what's going on, Dylan."

Drat. Why had I mentioned Eliot this morning? But Nicole had seen Mason harassing him at the game too. And she followed up on every possible lead. She was very good at her job.

"Is he still at the station?" I said.

"I don't know. I haven't seen him since. That's over three hours ago now. Like I said, I have no clue, Dylan. I was actually hoping you could give me a hint here."

"I've been at work all day too, Robbie. Just got off. Was hoping to have a chat with Eliot myself about something." My eyes shifted when I said that. She noticed.

"It's about that fire last night, isn't it?" she said. She started scooping my favorite flavor, Chocolate Monkey, into a waffle cone. "He was talking about it. Wondering how it got started, how long it took to put out. And it made me nervous. I mean, don't they say arsonists like to talk about their crimes? That they like the attention? Don't they even call 9-1-1 sometimes, then stick around to watch?"

"Um, I don't really know for sure about that," I told her as she handed me the cone. "I don't know any arsonists personally." I tried to smile, but it was too hard, so I licked the cone instead. "Maybe I'll run into him on my way home. Got to go. There's some sort of a summer shindig happening at Monica's place tonight. Starts around seven thirty. My mom and Brent and Gran and Buddy and I are invited. Mom has the whole weekend off for a change. Sweet, eh?"

I was rambling, talking too fast. Robbie just stood there nodding and frowning.

"So catch you later. Hope Eliot shows up for his shift tomorrow. I better get home now."

"I hope so too, Dylan," Robbie said with a quick wave. Then the door tinkled. Four girls, younger than me. All giggling tweens. Robbie would have to start scooping or making milkshakes. When I smiled at them, they giggled even harder.

I walked out of the Scoop Coupe. But I wasn't going home just yet. First I had to make a stop at Eliot's place.

Chapter Nine

On the way over, my phone rang. It was Monica. Of course. It was six thirty. I was already sort of late. I'd told her I would call as soon as I got home, so I knew exactly what this one was about.

"Dylan? Are you home yet?"

"Sorry, you got the wrong number," I told her.

"Ha-ha. Why were you ignoring my texts? Last I heard you were getting a ride home from Jonas, right?"

"Sorry, my phone was on mute. And I needed a snack, so I got dropped by the Coupe. Got a Chocolate Monkey waffle cone. Eating it now. Are you jealous?"

"So you're going home now, right?" Totally ignoring my stab at humor.

"On the way," I told her. Which was mostly the truth.

"Okay, try to be at our place for seven thirty, Dylan. I don't want you to miss a thing."

"Don't worry," I said. "Mom's driving, and she's never late."

"Cool," she said. "As long as you're on time. I don't want you to miss the surprise. It's at eight on the dot!"

"It's a *surprise* party?" I said. "Who's it for?"

"You never listen to me, do you?" she said, then hung up on me. And I totally deserved it too.

By then I'd reached Eliot's street. I stood for a moment in front of his rundown little house with all the random junk stowed on the front porch. Always the same. I knocked on the door and then walked right in. He never locked his door.

The tiny kitchen was a disaster area. The entire house seemed to get worse every time I dropped by. Like his dad, Eliot was a junk collector, a dumpster diver. Because you never knew what you could fix up and sell on Kijiji.

There was something that actually did look out of place though. In the middle of the kitchen floor was a greasy-looking Blue Jays cap. I'd seen that someplace before. Weird.

"Yo, you home, buddy?" I called out. The place was dead quiet. I wondered if I should check his room or just leave it alone. Then I heard something like a muffled snore.

His bedroom door was open slightly. I peered in, and yep, there he was, sprawled face down on the bed, fully dressed and sound asleep. He still had his shoes on too. And there was soot on the bottom of his frigging sneakers! I shoved the last bite of cone into my mouth and chewed it up as I stood there listening to him snore. Sleeping soundly like maybe he hadn't slept last night? With Eliot's lifestyle, you never could tell. What the heck was going on around here anyway?

The entire way home I wondered if Nicole and Stanley had noticed Eliot's shoes. Duh, of course they had. I'd automatically started checking everyone's shoes myself, ever since Stanley had pointed out the soot on Mason's sneakers. But why did everyone seem to have sooty shoes all of a sudden? Not really everyone. Just people *I* knew! How bizarre was that?

And yeah, by then I was running really late. It was another twenty minutes from Eliot's place back to our apartment. It was already past seven by then. And I still needed to take a shower. There would be food at the party, since it was a surprise party. But for who? Did I need to take a gift? I kind of hoped my mom had thought of that for me. I started jogging.

I was unlocking our apartment door by seven twenty-five. Turned out I didn't have to. It was already open, and Mom was sitting there staring at me.

"Gran and Buddy are there already. Brent is too. You realize this is a *surprise* party, right, Dylan? For Monica's younger brother, Oliver? He's turning thirteen today."

"Of course I knew that," I said. "Oliver's thirteen today."

"So what did you get him?" Mom raised her eyebrows at me.

"I stopped off at the Coupe after work and got him a gift certificate. Perfect, right?" Only half a lie—I actually *did* stop off at the Coupe.

"Good plan." She nodded and smiled. I bolted to my bedroom and flung off my clothes.

"Jeez," I yelled. "I must have left the certificate on the counter when I was talking to Robbie. We'll have to stop off on the way so I can pick it up."

"Then you'd better hurry!"

My phone was vibrating madly. I ignored it. I practically dove into the shower and didn't even bother to lather up. Too bad if I was stinky. I applied a good dose of pit lube and started yanking on my cargo shorts and Blue Jays T-shirt. Fastest time *ever*.

But why did everyone have sooty shoes? What the heck was I missing here?

Mom waited out in her car with the engine running while I ran into the Scoop Coupe. And there was Eliot, scooping cones like everything was normal. His nap must've worked out for him. I sidled up to him behind the counter and started filling out a gift certificate for twenty-five bucks. I had done it tons of times when I worked there.

"Dude, what happened to you today? What did they say to you at the station?" I scribbled Oliver's name on the certificate, then dropped a five and a twenty into the till.

Eliot frowned and shrugged. "Turns out they had no evidence to charge me with anything," he half-whispered. "Just some soot on my shoes. Which means nothing."

"What's with the soot though, Eliot?" I needed to know.

Eliot just started scooping another cone. There was a long lineup in the shop. Parents were beginning to look annoyed with me, standing there and *not* scooping cones. Little kids were squirming and whining. Outside, the car horn honked twice. I had to leave.

"Later," I told Eliot. "And I want to hear all the details. From start to finish."

Chapter Ten

Mom took her regular shortcut along a bumpy road that ran parallel to the lake. It wasn't far from the spot where Monica and I had pulled the rowboat up onto the rock slab the day before.

We were only halfway to Monica's place when I spotted plumes of smoke above the treetops near the shoreline.

"Slow down, Mom," I told her and pointed.

There was no way I would ever forget what Stanley had said that morning. The whole "crispy critters" thing. And he and Nicole had both made it clear— no fires right now in this area. For any reason whatsoever. But, like they say, where there's smoke, there's fire.

"Oh no," Mom murmured as she pulled her car onto the gravel shoulder. "Not another brush fire. I'd better call 9-1-1."

"I'm going over to see what's happening," I told her. By then I was already out of the car.

"Wait, Dylan," she said as I slammed the door. "It might be dangerous."

In another second I was charging through the woods. I heard her car door slamming and her footsteps pounding on the trail behind me. I just kept on running, then stopped dead in my tracks. Mom caught up to me. We were standing about a hundred meters from a rundown little clapboard cottage. Flames danced out the windows. And there was an old lady on the ground. Old Mrs. Winston. Someone was leaning over her doing CPR. He had flaming red hair.

My mom gasped. "Jeb Wilder?" she whispered. "Wildfire."

"Jeb Wilder?" I had no idea who *he* was. All I knew was that this dude doing CPR was the same guy who'd spit at me the week before. The same guy whose grimy ballcap I'd seen on the floor at Eliot's place. The homeless dude who slept out in the woods. And if this fire didn't get put out fast, Mom was right. There really would be a wildfire.

This guy Jeb heard the sirens the same instant we did and looked up. And spotted us. Then sprang to his feet and vanished into the forest. Just left the old lady lying on the ground.

I ran straight over. No hesitation at all. I'd finally taken a first-aid course, which had made Monica very happy too. I started chest compressions with "Stayin' Alive" playing on a soundtrack in my brain. My mom was still frozen to the spot.

In my pocket my phone was vibrating. But I just kept pumping hard on Mrs. Winston's sternum. I didn't want this old lady to be dead. Except that her jaw was all slack and her face was gray. And her eyes were rolled back in her head. Only the white parts were showing. It wasn't looking good at all. I had no idea if Mom was beside me or behind me. I just kept up my pumping until the paramedics came crashing through the bushes with all their equipment, followed by a fire crew and Nicole and Stanley.

There were tears in my eyes the whole time. Even when they pushed me aside and took over. I did *not* want this old lady to be dead on my watch.

But she was.

When an ambulance leaves with a patient *without* turning on the siren, it's usually not a good sign. I stood on the edge of the clearing, all sooty and sweaty. I watched in a total daze as the firefighters poured water through Mrs. Winston's kitchen window. Mrs. Winston who would never be going home again. It totally sucked. And I felt like puking.

Nicole and Mom were on either side of me. Mom's arm was around my shoulder, and Nicole's was around my waist. My heart was still pounding fast, and my legs were all rubbery.

"Oh god, Dylan, I'm so sorry." Mom buried her face in my neck, which was awkward since I was so much taller than her now.

"Honestly, you did your best, Dylan, your *very* best. Everything you learned at that course you took," my godmother told me.

"But I didn't *do* anything," I murmured.

"Of course you did," they said together.

"All I did was pump. It was that other guy, that Jeb Wilder guy. He got her out of the house. He started the chest compressions. I just finished what he started. And it didn't work either, did it, because now—"

"Hold on a sec." Nicole was suddenly in cop mode. She dropped her arm and stepped in front of me. "You're saying Jeb Wilder was here?"

"Oh god, I nearly forgot," Mom said. "Yes. He was helping Mrs. Winston when we got here. I'm sure it was him.

You can't miss that wild red hair. But I thought he left town a long time ago."

"*Who* is Jeb Wilder?" I said. "I've seen that guy hanging around here. He tried to spit on me last week and chased me away."

"Your mom and I went to school with him," Nicole told me. "Everyone called him Wildfire. Kept getting into trouble with the police around here, so he dropped out and moved to the city. There were rumors that he had some mental health issues and was in hospital for a bit but wouldn't stay on his meds. Poor guy."

I knew what Nicole was thinking. I was thinking it too. Was Jeb Wilder the one who started that fire in the first place? And maybe the other one too? Maybe even all the other ones this season, including the grass fires?

"Look, I've got to go," Nicole said. "I've got to chase this lead, try to track Jeb down."

"Mom?" I said. "Can you just drop me off at home? Maybe you could explain to Monica. I'm not feeling so great. I just want to go and lie down for a while."

"Oh honey," Mom said. "Should I stay with you? I don't mind, you know."

"No, you should go to the party. Brent is waiting for you. But just take me home first, okay?"

"Of course. Come on, let's get going."

I couldn't wait to get home and change out of my sooty clothes.

But after that I wasn't really going to lie down. I was going to jump on my bike and head straight over to the Scoop Coupe to ask Eliot about that Blue Jays ball cap lying on his kitchen floor. He was hiding Jeb Wilder, and I wanted to know why.

Chapter Eleven

Okay, so I really wasn't feeling great. I hadn't lied about that. But I hadn't been upfront about why.

I thought about it as I biked to the Scoop Coupe. Sure, I'd done CPR on Mrs. Winston. Chest compressions. One hundred per minute. And I'd done them properly too. But I left out one very important step. Her chest wasn't rising. I should have been delivering rescue breaths. I didn't though, because I did *not* want to put my lips on a corpse's mouth. I knew it was totally wrong, leaving that part out. But I did it anyway.

And now? Well, now I felt I owed something to the spirit of Mrs. Winston. And to her family as well. I needed to try to find out who had started that fire in the first place. And I knew exactly where to look.

I flung open the door of the Scoop Coupe and stared at the ice-cream counter, trying to control the shakes that had suddenly overcome me. Shock or something? No clue. But I was ready to grab Eliot by the throat and make him tell me what the heck was going on.

Except he wasn't there anymore. Some other kid was scooping now. A girl I recognized from my school. A year younger than me.

"Where is he, Caitlin?" I said, probably a bit too loudly. "Is he in the back?"

Everyone in the store turned around to stare at me. I ignored them.

"Where's *Eliot*?" My voice was husky now. I almost felt like crying. "Just *tell* me."

"I don't *know*, Dylan," she said, looking scared. "He just…left. I'm finishing his shift for him. Robbie's in the back."

Just then Robbie stuck her head around the doorframe at the back of the shop.

"Eliot had to leave again," she told me. "Said it was an emergency. What could I say?"

"Thanks." I spun around and walked out.

And headed right for Eliot's place. Again.

For the first time ever, the door was locked. I started pounding hard, then kicking it with my sneaker. Harder and harder, taking all my frustrations out on that chipped gray door. Yelling Eliot's name and kicking, wishing it could be him instead, I was that angry. By the time Eliot opened the door, I was totally fried. All I could do was push my way inside. I noticed the ball cap wasn't on the floor. But the rest of the place was the exact same disaster area.

"Why did you leave work again, dude?" I said. "Because I know you were here just after six. I stood in your bedroom, looking at you. You were out cold. Then you went back to work. Now you're here *again*. You *were* at that fire last night. That's why there's soot on your shoes. So where *is* he, Eliot?"

Eliot gulped, then sat down hard on one of the mismatched kitchen chairs.

"Who are you talking about? He *who*?" He looked down at his knees. Gulped again. "How do you figure all this stuff out?" he said. "How did you even know that someone else was here? Who *are* you anyway? Sherlock freakin' Holmes?"

I pushed a heap of old papers off a chair and sat down.

"Look, you've been leaving a trail of clues everywhere. What am I supposed to think? That greasy baseball cap that was on the floor a couple of hours ago? It belongs to Jeb Wilder. AKA Wildfire. I know that for a fact because he went to school with my mom and Nicole. Now tell me what's going on."

Eliot just sat there staring at his hands. Then he looked up at me.

"Don't be mad at me, okay, Dylan? I mean, I really trust you now after everything that happened a few months ago. And I thought we were friends."

"We *are* friends! I got you a job at the Coupe, didn't I? And I'm always trying to protect your butt. But I'm starting to get *really* sick of it."

"Okay, okay," he said. "You don't have to be so harsh. Here's the story. Jeb Wilder showed up at my door a couple of weeks ago. My dad warned me that he might be coming."

"Your dad knows him too? Jeez, Eliot! How?"

"Well, *duh*, he went to school with Jeb too, back in the day. They both grew up here in Bridgewood. Then Jeb quit and split for the city. But he's always kept in touch with my dad. Calls him at the camp out west. Usually when he needs a few bucks." Eliot sighed. "So when he showed up at the door, what was I supposed to do? Send him away?"

He had a point. "So is this guy homeless or what?"

"Yeah. Down in the city he pretty much lives on the street. A dumpster diver. Kind of like me." He grinned then, almost proudly. "He came up here for the summer though. Likes to sleep in the woods. All he has is his backpack, you know. That's his pillow. I let him shower here and give him food too sometimes. And I've told him he can sleep here when the weather's bad, if he wants to. He knows the door's always open for him. I thought you of all people would understand."

Wow. I had it all wrong. Here I was judging Eliot again, just like everyone else in town.

"Sorry, man. I should have known you'd do the right thing. But why was your door locked just now?" I asked. "You've never locked it before."

"Because I was scared," Eliot said. "See, Jeb took off this afternoon. Said he needed to get somewhere and just left.

I didn't think much of it. He's always coming and going. I had a snooze and went to work."

"Yeah, so why did you *leave* work?"

"Because right after I got there, Jeb stuck his head in the back door of the Scoop Coupe and said to meet him at my place. Said he needed to tell me something really important. So I told Robbie I had to go. But when I got here he *wasn't* here. I don't know. I had the feeling something bad was going down. I've been waiting for him to come back ever since. But also kind of hoping he won't show up."

I sat there staring into space. Eliot thought I had all the answers. But I didn't have any. Yet. And I wasn't about to tell him what had just happened at poor Mrs. Winston's place either. I was pretty sure he'd be hearing about that soon enough.

"So what were you really doing out in the woods last night, dude?"

Eliot took a deep breath. "I went down there to chill with Jeb for a while. He likes the woods. Feels at home. We were lying on a rock by the shore, staring at the stars. It was cool."

"Seriously? With *that* sketchy guy?" I shook my head.

"Once you get to know him, he's not so bad. Anyway, I guess we fell asleep. We woke up when we heard somebody yelling. Then we spotted the flames and started stamping them out. When I heard the sirens, I got scared and took off for home. Jeb showed up a while later."

So that's why his shoes were filthy. That left only one other person with sooty shoes and no explanation.

"Okay, so where's Jeb now? What do you think happened to him?" I asked. I knew he'd been trying to save Mrs. Winston a while ago. But what was the "something really important" he had to tell Eliot?

"Honestly, no clue, dude," Eliot said.

"Look," I told him. "I'm outta here. It's getting late, and I have to work tomorrow. Promise me you won't go anywhere, okay? Trust me on this. Just stay right here and keep your door locked. Let Jeb in if he shows."

He shrugged. "Sure."

"Hey, Eliot," I said as I reached for the doorknob. "I'm glad you told me the truth. You have a lot of explaining to do to Robbie, and probably to Officer Vance and that Stanley guy too. But I've got your back, buddy. And man, I'm so glad that it wasn't you who started the fire. And that you tried to help put it out." I gave him a fist bump and took off. I heard the door lock behind me.

It was already twilight by then, and dark was falling fast. I figured the party would still be going strong though. I checked my phone. No messages. Monica was either really mad or understood completely. I'd find that out tomorrow.

But tonight I still had some work to do. I really needed to talk to this Wildfire guy, and I had a feeling I knew where he was hiding out.

Chapter Twelve

It wasn't very far from Eliot's place to the cottage where Monica and I had borrowed the rowboat. I knew the owners were at the party too. Oliver and the kid who lived at the cottage were friends. Nobody would even know I was using the boat tonight.

Like all good Boy Scouts, I had come prepared. I always carried an LED flashlight in my cargo pocket, along with my Leatherman multi-tool. Never knew when I'd need the stuff. I dropped my bike on the dock, climbed into the rickety rowboat and untied the rope. Then I grabbed the oars and started rowing. I was starting to get the hang of this.

I was headed for the flat rock where Jeb and Eliot had been stargazing the night before. Eliot said Jeb felt at home in the woods. I had a hunch he'd gone back there after running away from the fire scene this afternoon. That would have been after he'd told Eliot to meet him at home. He was probably hiding out now, terrified because Mom and I had spotted him.

As I rowed closer, I dug out my flashlight and started playing it along the shoreline. I was getting closer to Mrs. Winston's cottage. And I wasn't sure I wanted to see what was left of it. I felt sick enough already. As my light danced in the darkness, I heard a splash. An animal? Or something else? I shot the shaft of light toward a cottage dock, and the beam landed on someone's pale face—under the dock. Staring straight at me. There he was, crouched in the space just up from the waterline. Wildfire.

"Yo, Jeb," I called as I rowed a little closer. "Can I talk to you a sec?"

"Get out of here," he said. Just like the last time I'd run into him.

"Eliot sent me to look for you," I told him. "He's my friend."

Pause. "Oh yeah? He's a pretty good dude, I guess." His voice was softer now. "I know his dad."

"So I heard. Why are you hiding under the dock?"

"The police dog. I heard it barking in the woods. I think they're looking for me. They think I started the fires, but I *didn't*. I actually called 9-1-1 last night when we couldn't stamp out the fire."

"That was *you*?"

"Yeah, that was me. Eliot freaked when he heard the sirens, so he took off without his bike. I rode it up to the main drag, made the call, then went back to his place."

"You tried to save Mrs. Winston today. My mom and I saw you."

"The old lady? Yeah. I yanked her out of the house through the back door. She was already dead though. I've seen enough dead bodies on the street to know one by now. But I tried anyway."

I felt a big weight lift off my shoulders.

"I tried to save her too," I told him. "I wonder how the fire started. Maybe she fell asleep and a cigarette fell out of her hand? Who knows? She was a heavy smoker. Everyone in town knew that."

"Yeah. Bad habit. Those things can kill you." He made a weird sound, almost a laugh.

"Come on out of there, Jeb. Go back to Eliot's place. The door's locked, but he's there waiting for you. He's worried about you."

"Oh yeah? He's actually worried? He really is a cool young lad."

Then I took a chance. "Eliot mentioned that you needed to tell him something important. Was it about the fire last night? Did you maybe see someone else down there?"

"How did you know that?" Jeb said.

"Just a hunch."

"Yeah, I couldn't see so good with only the moonlight. But someone was definitely taking off from there really fast. Someone on a bike, wearing a ballcap. I just don't know if I should go to the cops."

"That's your decision," I told him. "But why did you tell the cops that it was Mason Bates who started the fire?"

Long pause. "What do you mean? I never told the cops it was Mason Bates. Who is Mason Bates?"

"Wow, thanks," I said. "You might have just helped me figure things out. Later, Jeb."

I needed to get home. I felt pretty sure I knew what was going on now, but I needed solid proof.

As I was gliding through the darkness toward the dock, I heard a dog bark. I knew that bark. A flashlight came on and practically blinded me. Nicole was standing at the end of the dock. Her partner Prince, the German shepherd, strained on his leash.

"*There* you are!" she said. "You had everyone worried sick. Why don't you check your phone once in a while?"

"Sorry," I said. "I must have left it in my room."

"Well, hurry and tie up the boat. Then grab your bike and let's get you home before your mom loses her mind."

I was in no hurry to get home now. I was dreading the "surprise party" that was probably waiting for me. Nicole must have been really mad, because she didn't say anything as she drove. Prince was in the backseat. I could feel him panting on my neck. When we were nearly there I risked one question.

"Did Mom think something bad happened to me, Nic?"

"Well, what do *you* think she thought, Dylan?" She stared straight through the windshield. "You weren't answering her texts or Monica's, so she went home. You weren't there. Your bike was gone too. And she knew how upset you were about Mrs. Winston when she dropped you off. Plus, weird stuff tends to happen to you, right? So figure it out. You're usually pretty good at that."

Tears jumped into my eyes, and I brushed them away quickly. I wondered how I'd even be able to face anyone when I got back to our apartment.

When we reached the sixth floor the apartment door was already wide open. When I walked through the doorway Mom just jumped up and ran over to me and started hugging me hard. Monica was there too. She'd been crying, I could tell. And Brent was there, and Gran and Buddy too. All staring at me. Complete silence for a count of ten. Then everyone started yacking at the exact same second.

"Oh god, where were you, Dylan?" Monica, hugging me harder than Mom.

"How could you do this to us? What were you thinking?" Gran, of course.

"We were all really worried about you, buddy!" Brent.

"So sorry to hear what happened with poor Mrs. Winston. How horrible." Buddy Dalton.

"She was already dead," I said. That shut them all up pretty fast.

"How do you know that?" Nicole said. "There hasn't even been an autopsy yet."

"Because Jeb Wilder told me. You know, Wildfire?"

"What? We looked all over the place for him after the fire today. Even Prince couldn't track him down."

"Yeah, well, he's been around, you know. He was hiding under a dock when I met up with him a while ago. And he's seen dead bodies before. He says he's sure Mrs. Winston was already dead when he dragged her out of the house. But he tried CPR anyway."

"So where is he now?" Nicole said. "And what were you doing out in that rowboat?"

"I have no clue where he is," I told her.

"You were out in the *dark* in a *rowboat*?" Mom practically screeched. "*Why,* Dylan? What is this all about? Geez!"

"I wore a life jacket, and I had a flashlight," I told her. "Really, I'm okay. I just needed some air. It's been a long day. But I'm really sorry that I worried you all so much. And now I just want to go to bed, okay? Goodnight, everybody."

Then I walked straight down the hallway to my room and locked my door.

Chapter Thirteen

I wasn't going to sleep yet though. Because I had one thing left to do first. Figure out how to make a lock pick out of a soda can. There were always a couple of empty ones on the desk in my room. And my Leatherman multi-tool had a pair of scissors and a great knife. So I got right to work. Awesome what you can find out how to do on the Internet.

From two soda cans I managed to make eight lock picks. Then I wasted two of them practicing on a padlock I had in my desk drawer. Got it first try the second time around though. And I still had six left. Sweet.

The next morning at work I was going to break into Jonas's locker and check out his backpack. He was the only employee who used a lock. I figured that guy had to be hiding something.

The next morning I got up early, even though my shift started at ten. I wanted to check something out before work.

At breakfast I was quiet and ate fast. Mom and Gran were staring at me, but I answered all their questions with a yes or no, so they left me alone. I only had to tell them once that I didn't feel like talking about what had happened the day before. Mom offered to give me a lift to work since I still looked tired, but I turned her down. Said the fresh air would do me good. Parents love it when you say stuff like that.

By nine thirty I was at the lodge, locking up my bike. I took a stroll around the grounds to scope out the fire pits. And yeah, I was *right*. I thought I'd remembered them being fully enclosed. There was no soot or ashes or charred wood spilling out of them that Jonas could have tracked in on his work boots. No way. And there was a *fire ban*. So Granitewood Lodge wasn't allowing any campfires anyway, even to toast marshmallows.

As I was heading back to the lodge I spotted Jonas crossing the lawn with a couple of other guys who did maintenance on the property. They were all carrying Tim Hortons cups. They usually liked to sit on the dock for a while before their shift started.

Jonas looked at me sort of funny, then gave a friendly wave, and I waved back.

"Hey, dude, you're early," he yelled. "What are you doing out here anyway? Thinking of joining the big boys on the outside? Work on your baseball muscles?"

"Huh, that's pretty funny, Jonas," I said.

The other two guys started laughing. I gave them a weak smile. I knew they thought I had a pretty lame job, working the front desk and being stuck inside all day while they got to do things like drive the lodge speedboat to take waterskiing guests for spins around the lake.

I still had fifteen minutes. The locker room was deserted. I dug one of the picks out of my pocket and wiggled it into the padlock. The thing got stuck and I had to wiggle it out, and after that it tore, of course. Then the door opened and one of the dining-room servers came in. Hannah, a friend of mine.

"Morning, Dylan," Hannah said. "Whoa. Usually you show up one minute before your shift."

"Yeah, ha. I guess I woke up early," I told her.

She grabbed something from her locker and slammed it shut.

"Big change for you, isn't it?" she said with a grin. "See ya later."

"See ya." As soon as she was gone I slipped the second pick in and wiggled it around, just like I'd practiced. No good. I needed two picks for this one. I inserted a second one and started to tug carefully, holding my breath the entire time. And then I heard it. That lucky click.

I whipped Jonas's backpack out of his locker and unzipped it. I could feel the sweat dripping in my pits now. Swimsuit, wallet, half-empty water bottle. Extra T-shirt, pair of work socks, pair of work shorts. Extra pack of smokes. And there on the bottom—bingo.

Bang! The locker-room door hit the wall.

"Can I help you out with something, O'Connor?"

When I spun around Jonas was staring at me, eyes narrowed. Then he stuck his head back out into the hallway.

"Hey, Mr. Hillier," he called. "Can you come in here for a second? There's something you really need to see."

Chapter Fourteen

I was sitting in a chair in Mr. Hillier's office, armpit sweat seeping down to my waist by then, not saying a word. Truth was, I was happy when Jonas called in Mr. Hillier. I thought I was a goner when he caught me. Then he surprised me again when he told Mr. Hillier that he actually *would* actually prefer if the cops got involved.

When Officer Donohue showed up a while later, he half-grinned when he spotted me. I'd been in trouble with him before.

"Fancy meeting you here, Dylan O'Connor. How unusual. What's happened *this* time?" he asked Mr. Hillier.

Jonas was sitting in the chair beside me with a super-smug grin on his face. His invisible halo was practically glowing. I said nothing.

"Well, one of my employees, Jonas here, caught Dylan going through his backpack in the locker room before work. Dylan must have jimmied his lock."

"With this pick I made from a soda can last night," I said, holding one up. "Cool, huh?"

They all stared at me, shocked.

"You actually admit you did all this?" Officer Donohue asked.

"Yep. But I had a very good reason. I think you should ask Jonas what he's got in that backpack, Officer."

I pointed to Mr. Hillier's desk, where the pack was sitting. Then my gaze shifted to Jonas's face. His eyes were extremely wide now.

"Well, *duh*. What do you think I have? All the stuff I might need for work. T-shirt, swimsuit, extra work socks, shorts—"

"Matches. Barbecue lighter. Tin of lighter fluid."

Officer Donohue and Mr. Hillier were frowning now.

"What do you need all that for, son?" the officer asked.

Long pause. "Well, I don't like to admit it, but I do smoke, you know. And I didn't want my boss to find out."

Mr. Hillier just shrugged. "Lots of kids your age smoke. Dumb habit, but not my problem as long as they don't do it on Lodge property."

"So what about the other items? Were you planning on lighting some barbecues sometime soon?" Officer Donohue asked.

Jonas swallowed hard. "Oh…well…I, uh…bought an extra lighter the other day. And some fluid. Just in case the one I'm using here runs out, you know? We light the barbecues up most days. For the kids who want hot dogs for lunch. You know, the kids in the daycare program. While their parents are off having fun. And we can't do it on sticks over a campfire, you know. Because of the fire ban." His smile was a bit wobbly.

"So why does that lighter in your backpack have a Granitewood Lodge logo on it then?" I asked him. "You didn't maybe steal it from the lodge, did you? And the fluid too? Says *extreme danger* on the can. And *highly flammable*.

Why would you even steal something from a great boss like Mr. Hillier? And why is there soot on your boots? You know, since campfires are banned and everything."

We all looked down at his boots. Wow, did I love the awkward silence that was filling that room.

"I think you'd better come with me, Jonas," Officer Donahue said. "To answer a few more questions. Okay with you, Mr. Hillier?"

"Of course," he said, nodding. He wouldn't even look at Jonas now. "Do what you have to. There are plenty of other employees here to cover for him."

Jonas didn't even try to protest. He looked totally stunned and close to tears as he followed Officer Donahue and his backpack out the door.

Mr. Hillier stared at me, half-smiling. "Dylan, can you stick around here for a few minutes? I think we need to talk."

"Sure thing, Mr. Hillier," I said.

I got a bit of a talking-to about invasion of privacy and whatnot. But I wasn't really in trouble. Mr. Hillier knew my motives were good. Sometimes I went overboard when I needed to know the truth. Even if it got me in a bit of trouble sometimes.

Mom invited everyone over for dinner that night. When Nicole arrived she told us that Jonas had caved, admitting to starting the first fire in the woods and making an anonymous call blaming Mason.

And he did it for the dumbest reason ever. Not that there's ever a *good* reason for starting a wildfire anywhere. He wanted to get Mason in trouble. He was still holding a grudge against Mason for being so successful when his own baseball career had fizzled out. Mason had given him a hard time just like he did with everyone else. But finally Jonas had decided to teach him a lesson in his own warped way, by ratting him out to the cops for something he didn't do.

During his questioning at the station, Jonas even tried to blame Mason again. But that argument went nowhere with the cops. Then he told them that at least he'd tried to stomp it out after he started it, because he felt bad about starting it in the first place, and then it got out of hand. Of course, Officer Donahue had absolutely no sympathy for him.

Jonas *hadn't* started the second fire, the one on Friday evening though. The Fire Marshall's Office was still investigating the cottage fire, but it was looking like it might have been caused by careless smoking. Mrs. Winston likely died of smoke inhalation before Jeb pulled her out of the cottage, but the autopsy would confirm.

"And you'll never believe it, but Jeb actually showed up at the station this afternoon. All clean, hair brushed. I'm still in shock," Nicole said. "He looked pretty good."

"Maybe he's turning over a new leaf. And I don't mean the ones you sleep on!" Buddy could always be counted on for a corny joke.

"I wonder what's going to happen to him now," Mom asked. "He's getting too old to live the wandering life."

"It's actually really good news," Nicole said. "He has decided to stay up here. He'll move in with Eliot so he won't have to live outside. And he's going to start looking for a job."

"We always need servers at Rocky's Roadhouse," Mom said. "I'd definitely hire him."

"Sweet," I said. "He's a nice guy. He really is. I met him out on the lake last night, remember?"

Deb Loughead is a regular contributor to the Orca Currents series. *Payback, The Snowball Effect, Caught in the Act* and *Rise of the Zombie Scarecrows* also feature Dylan and his friends. Deb lives in Toronto, Ontario. For more information, visit debloughead.ca.

Also by
Deb Loughead

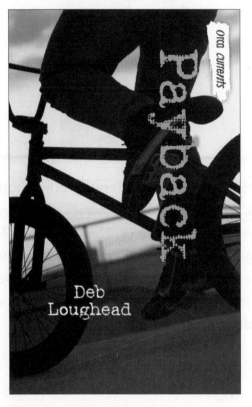

9781459814691 PB

"I don't even want to hear another word about that, Dylan," Mom told me, shaking her head. "Eat up, everyone. Don't let Gran's awesome oven-baked fried chicken get cold."

"And pass around that potato salad instead of hogging it all yourself, mister," said Gran, winking at me. I knew she really meant it though.

Later, when Monica and I were sitting out on the balcony to get away from everyone inside, I mentioned something I'd been thinking about all day.

"You know what? I think I'd like to take some flowers over to Mrs. Winston's property. Maybe after work tomorrow. Leave them under a tree or something. What do you think?"

"I think that's the sweetest thing ever," Monica told me. "I'll pick up a bouquet in town, then meet you at the lodge after you're done work. We can take them over together."

"Honestly, you're the best," I said. I hugged her and kissed the top of her head.

Then I reached under my chair and handed her the plastic bag I'd stowed there after I got home from work. On my bike. No ride from Jonas today.

"What's this?" she said.

"Open it," I told her, and she did.

"*The Definitive Guide to Birds of Eastern North America.* Where did you *find* this? I've totally been dying to get my hands on a copy!"

"Yeah, I stopped at the bookstore on my way home from work. Apparently this is the guide that all the serious birdwatchers have."

"Really? You actually thought of doing this yourself?"

"Well, yeah, I mean, just because *I* think birds are boring and birdwatching is a drag, doesn't mean that…um…what I meant is…"

"Dylan!" Monica said, patting my arm. "Just stop talking before you ruin the moment!"

Yup. Monica was right, yet again.

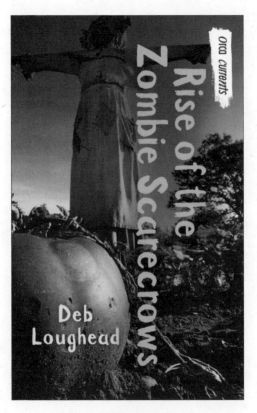

9781459809963 PB

Orca *currents*

For more information on all the books
in the Orca Currents series, please visit
orcabook.com.